This Book Belongs To:

....

D1537672

The Best
EASTER
EGG
HUNT
EVER

This edition published by Parragon Books Ltd in 2017
and distributed by

Parragon Inc.
440 Park Avenue South, 13th Floor
New York, NY 10016
www.parragon.com

Written by Dawn Casey   Illustrated by Katy Hudson

ISBN 978-1-4748-9971-0

Printed in China

The Best EASTER EGG HUNT EVER

Written by **Dawn Casey**
Illustrated by **Katy Hudson**

PaRRagon

Bath • New York • Cologne • Melbourne • Delhi
Hong Kong • Shenzhen • Singapore

On a warm spring day, in the tall green grass,
a little gray rabbit was sniffing the air.

It was Easter Sunday.
It was egg-hunt time.
Mother Rabbit said,
"There are lots of eggs to find."

"There are **stripy** eggs and **spotted** eggs, sky-blue eggs, **pale pink** eggs, and eggs as bright as **buttercups!**"

"I want a special egg," said Rabbit.
And off she hopped to see what she could find.

Down in the barnyard, Chick
was hopping around a haystack.
"Please help me, Rabbit," he
cheeped. "I can't reach that egg."
Rabbit hopped onto the haystack
in one leap. Nestled in the hay
was a sky-blue Easter egg.

"I don't have much," said Chick.
"But I can give you some feathers
to say thank you."
Rabbit tucked the feathers into
her basket, and off she hopped.

Over in the meadow,
Butterfly had found a tiny egg,
as bright as a buttercup.

The flowers waved in the breeze,
and the air was full of bees.

Rabbit hopped with happiness.
She followed a buzzing bee and
nibbled a yellow-green leaf.
She picked a bunch of spring flowers.

"Oh," Rabbit laughed. "I almost forgot about finding an egg." And off she hopped. . . .
Up on the hillside, lambs bounced and bounded.

Rabbit looked for an egg in the treetops

and in the hedges.

She found some scraps of sheep's wool stuck in the brambles,
but she didn't find a single egg.

So off she hopped.

In the sunlit woodland,
Rabbit heard a squeak.
"I can't dig up this egg!"
said Mouse.
"I'll help," said Rabbit.
"I can dig."

SCRAPE.

SCRATCH.

DIG.

BURROW.

"Wow!" breathed Mouse, looking at the giant egg.

"It's bigger than our whole mousehole!"
And Mouse gave Rabbit some tasty grass
to say thank you.

Rabbit's ears drooped.
"Mouse found a very special egg,"
she sighed. "But I haven't found
any eggs."

Rabbit didn't feel like hopping anymore. She sat down by the duck pond.

And there, by the water's edge, was an egg. But it wasn't big or bright, spotted or stripy, pink or blue or yellow.

It was small

and dull

and white.

"It doesn't look very special," said Rabbit.

Rabbit touched the egg with her paw.
"Oh," she whispered. "It's warm!"

A cold breeze blew. Rabbit shivered.
"Don't worry, little egg," she said. "I'll keep you warm."
And Rabbit emptied out her basket.

She took the stalks of grass and
the sweet flowers and
wove them together.

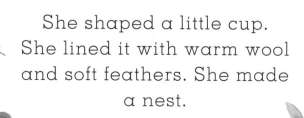

She shaped a little cup.
She lined it with warm wool
and soft feathers. She made
a nest.

And when the egg was safe and warm,
Rabbit curled up close by.
She was tired after her long day.
Soon she was fast asleep.

Peep! Peep!

What was that noise?

Peep! Peep!

It was coming from inside the egg.

The egg wobbled and rocked in the nest,
and all the time, it went,

Peep! Peep! Peep!

Until, CRICK! Out came a beak!

And CRACK! Out came . . .

"A duckling!"

"Quack! Quack!"
Mother Duck swam to shore.
"Oh, thank you!" she said.
"My egg! I've been looking for it all day."

Rabbit smiled.
"I'm glad I found this egg," she said.

"It's the most wonderful Easter egg of all."

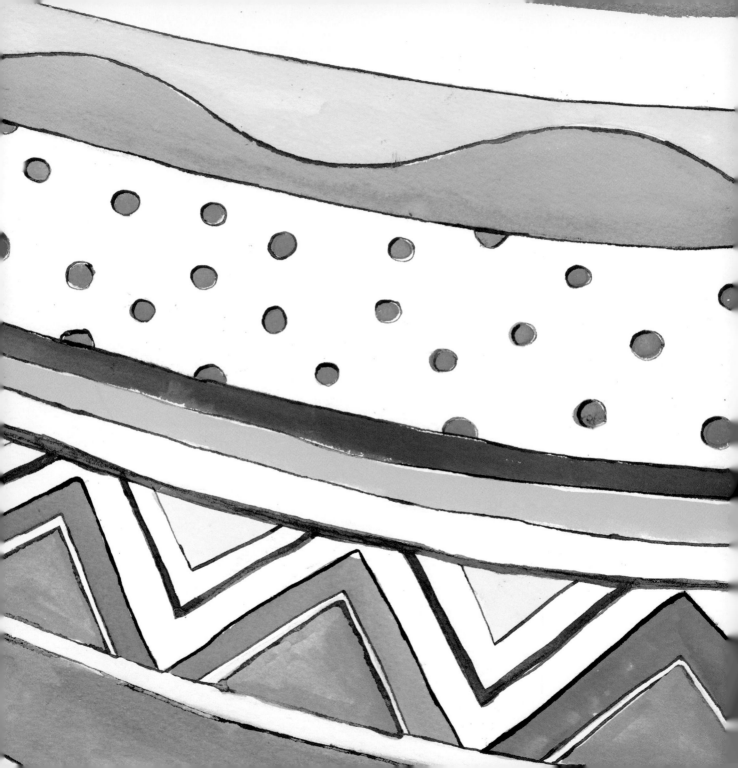

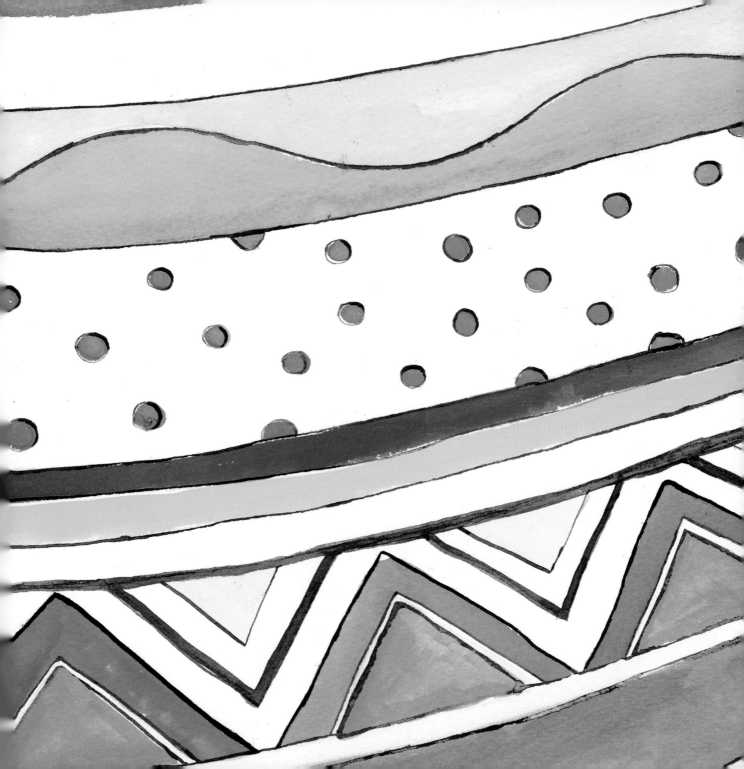